The Million-Year
centipede
or, Liquid structures

the million-year
centipede
or, liquid structures

eckhard gerdes

Published by Raw Dog Screaming Press
Hyattsville, MD

First Paperback Edition

Cover: Jennifer C. Barnes
Book design: M. Garrow Bourke
Interior Illustrations: Jim the Innocent

Printed in the United States of America

ISBN 978-1-933293-35-6

Library of Congress Control Number: 2007922467

www.rawdogscreaming.com

For my three sons, Sterling, Ludwig and Ulysses. May you forever surf successfully on the liquid structures of your own lives. I'll man the harpoons to keep the centipedes off your boards.

introduction

My WIFE, KIDS AND I recently moved to California. I was forced
by budget constraints to jettison some 80% of all the paperwork I
had accumulated over the past thirty years. Going through dozens
and dozens of boxes of yellowed receipts, letters from forgotten
acquaintances, irrelevant bank statements, and outdated tax papers
was interesting enough. Ticket stubs from concerts I had once attended, hotel matches from trips I'd taken, postcards to and from
my family brought back memories long buried beneath the flotsam
and jetsam of daily existence, forgotten in the hurry of trying to
scurry fast enough to make a living.

Also in the move, I became reacquainted with my old writings,
many of them so old that their friendship predates my family itself. These old friends, I thought at first, would be wearisome com-
panions now, and for the most part I was right. My hundreds of
bad adolescent rhyming poems, written in high school, where they
should have been left, resurfaced. Hopefully they will sink again just
as quickly. Old short stories that had failed in workshop attempts

during one of my many attempts at an MFA (which I eventually earned at the School of the Art Institute of Chicago—bless the place!) still failed now. But one work in particular called to me— my first novel.

Many years ago, after having been taken to task for my poetry one time too many, I actually heard what one teacher said to me: he told me my poems seemed to have a narrative impulse, and perhaps I'd be better at writing fiction. Perhaps he's right, I thought at the time, and so I began. That was back in 1978. I named the first novel *The Million-Year Centipede; or, Liquid Structures*, knowing only slightly what I wanted to write about. Now, of course, 27 years and a dozen novels later, I have come to the Beckettian revelation that subject ≠ matter. But, for that first novel, I felt I had something to say. I'm sure many of such first novels, especially by 19-year-olds, have a feel of being the writer's "things to get off my chest, part one." In that sense, mine was no exception. But in other ways, I think it is.

Million-Year Centipede is, if nothing else, a novel about hero-worship. It is also a thinly-veiled *roman à clef* about a trip I took to find my then-hero, Jim Morrison, the leader of the rock band The Doors. I had bought into keyboardist Ray Manzarek's dubious claim that Morrison faked his own death and is still alive somewhere (a claim he seems to still be proffering and profiting from—see his recent novel). I *studied* Morrison's lyrics the way any psycho fan studies his idol's work. In particular, I studied one of his longest and most significant pieces, "The Celebration of the Lizard," in which he suggests that after seven years of exile he will return to the land of the "fair and the strong and the wise." Assuming, with his love of Los Angeles being a given (his love song for the city, "L.A. Woman," proving the case), that he meant L.A., I decided to travel there and be present for his what-I-thought-would-be-triumphant return. So, on the seventh anniversary of his death (that is, his alleged "disappearance"), I flew to L.A., checked into the seven-dollar a night transient hotel that shared a name with and was pictured on the Doors' album *Morrison Hotel*. There I lay in wait, expecting something to happen. Nothing did. Or did it?

Coming away from that experience, I began to question the nature of blind faith and hero worship. I decided never again to lay faith in anyone or anything outside of myself until she or it or whatever had proven herself or itself to me. I became a skeptic, and my life has been a much healthier one as a result. Bob Dylan said it well: "Don't follow leaders—feed the parking meters." Putting a quarter in the slot doesn't mean you have to buy into the philosophy of those who installed the meters. Dishing out a few bucks for an album doesn't make the singer a holy man. Wake up! Think for yourself. That's the ultimate message of the story of Wakelin and *The Million-Year Centipede*.

Eckhard Gerdes
Menifee, California
31 January 2005

chapter one

A CENTIPEDE HAS A million years to discover

    uncover the welded secret of

love.

       I have today
          today
                only
         today.

                            Quiet Alone
                            (at peace)

i awaken
  wake up
                alone alone.
                      It is for me today

Today

to   find

to   discover

         uncover why

     (in my

     mind)

to   gather

         together   Data

                                 the data necessary
                                 Minimal

love.

         for survival

              for   my
              survival

                        minimal.

                              I awe

                              awaken

                                 mustmustmustneed

Alone   to save   my mind)   sanity

                        life.   Need.

NEED TO AWAKEN

URGENTURGENTURGENTURGENT

alarm: RRRRRNG!

URGENT ....…......MISSION————today

today

only

today

(those who do not succeed fail)

DEATHSANE

DEATHSANITY

DEATH   riskriskrisk

SANITY

SANE

ITY

IT

The Million-Year Centipede

IABCDEFGH

IJKLMIJOPQRSTUVWXYZ

IJKLM

IN

IN

SANIN
SANIJKLM
SANIN
SANIT
SANIN
SANITY
SANIN
SANE

              INSANE

DEATH

                         riskriskrisk.

             INSANE

(the omnipresent duality of risk)

those who die cease to live

those who die

those who..................

..........die..............

..........die

Die

the die is cast...death is cast as risk.

URGENT:REPEAT:URGENT:REPEAT:URGENT--------------

--------------awaken.

NEED TO AWAKEN.

NEED   TO   AWAKEN!

TO   LIVE

ALIVE.

NEEDBLEEDSPEEDFREEDBREEDCREEDSEEDDEED

DEED

DEADDEADDEADDEAD.

ALARM:;URGENT:(DEADDEADDEAD;)...

THERE, is a need, to;; awake. n.

the reis: an eedtoa (Wake) ; N.

NSEW.

awaken...

(saneundead).

the risk shall

will

must

can

be overcome.

Sane Undead.

Mustmustmustneed

Alone.

Quiet Alone

(at peace)

i awaken.

⁂

He will not open his eyes. He fears the sight he is still unaccustomed to, though it persists night after night. He feels the dampness of his pillow on his cheek, an unnatural dampness that he will not understand.

Quietly, alone, he breathes a tear in the unnatural abandonment he knows is merely an untangled remain of what has again happened. Without opening his eyes he gently lifts himself from his pillow.

Slowly, meticulously, he systematically initiates his eyes subconsciously to what again he is to see. Compensating for the fear-produced perpetual light in the small room, he feels himself prepared. He opens his eyes cautiously.

He finds the sight difficult to stomach but, for the first time, controls his urge to vomit. The pillow is soaked with his blood.

⁂

Noon. He has eaten a quick breakfast of raw noodles and apricot nectar. He is afraid to open the window drapes of his apartment. This is a fear which pervades even to the fortieth floor of the high-rise in which he lives. It creeps in like a poisonous gas through the cracks in the door and the vents in the wall. It is this poison which has paralyzed him—with fear. He ritualistically turns on one of the few items which clothes his scantily-clad room. Perhaps today the news will be different. Perhaps... He doubts it.

Briefly, the television sputters and fizzes in complaint. Then the jumbles of horizontal lightning-bolts transform themselves into a close-focus view of a man reading a piece of paper. He appears to be in his middle thirties, white Caucasian male with shoulder-length well-groomed hair. He sports a small Hitleresque moustache in the style presently popular. He wears a high-collared green velvet vest over a collarless orange ruffled shirt. This is typically neat and conservative. *Fool*, thinks Wakelin to himself. *Fools, all of them.*

"...and the death toll attributed to the interference so far totals almost 15,000."

This had been going on for a long time. Somewhere between a dozen and a hundred a night every night for the past numerous months.

He had had friends...

☢

A dark red light pulsates in a steady beat. A smaller, black light, in the eye of the red light, pulsates irregularly to the lead guitar of rock and roll music.

Simple but diversionary, the dual-pulsator engrosses him after a minor combination of valium, whiskey, and marijuana.

He turns his attention to the oscilloscope, which he has set for an intense combination of many thin green lines, gyrating and dancing to the rhythm pouring forth from his stereo.

He feels very much alone.

He opens up his mind, laying bare buried levels of raw emotion. He is shocked to find predominantly one *feeling* pervading his consciousness-fog. Pain. The word itself hurts to consider. *Pain.*

18

His pain. Fighting it, he focuses on stupidity, aware that ignorance is an easy cure-all. For now, he has again suppressed his pain. Turned it out from himself into channels leading elsewhere—where, it didn't matter—just *away*.

⁂

It was all here,

        save me.

It came.

It left.

It laughed.

It shrugged.

        It rode the whitewater;

        It rode the stallion;

        It rode.

Perhaps riding was enough.

            Creation came and went.

            Everything was here—for a while.

Everything.

        Everybody was here to bid hello;farewell.

                Why?

It was all here,

        save me.

            I was elsewhere, riding my own steed.

⁂

Riding this thought, he allows himself out of his stupor, out of reflection, into the very heart of the mirror itself. He stares blankly out at the world, not absorbing yet containing his environment. He *is* the mirror, that human aspect of detachment and unconscious portrait, unfathomable and unapproachable.

He feels himself looked at, yet never into—the deeper the examination, the farther behind oneself one sees.

He is safe, for he is unseen. This thought reassures him. He must make preparations for what is to occur today. He has defeated his fear.

☙

Once more, he considers the blood on his pillow, which greets him like a silent alarm each morning. He cannot find any traces upon his person—he understands, though, that it comes out of him, out of his subconscious—the subconscious that is being ripped to shreds by the bare-toothed revenge of his difference. He realizes that, in its own way, his subconscious is experiencing a long and painful death and, in its struggle for survival, it is attempting to assert its control over his whole person, over his whole world. Whether he sweats or spits blood, he decides, matters as much as whether he can be held responsible for the deaths over the past months. Both may originate and emanate from a like source, but the source realizes little of why or how. These, ultimately, are those questions which need answers in order for his sanity and life to remain intact. He fears reality but, even moreso, he fears distortion. He fears himself.

chapter two

A CENTIPEDE, MOVING SLOWLY so as seemingly to take a million years, crawled up the thin metallic pole that, on a larger scale, appeared as one leg of the four upon which Wakelin's school-desk rested.

Wakelin marveled quietly at this layering of legs—a hundred upon one of four. He watched the creature's slow progress up the leg, around the corner, and onto the plateau upon which he rested his arms. He continued to watch as his mind reveled upon what occurred the evening before.

He had called up his girlfriend, who had been avoiding him recently. Bluntly, she had told him she had met someone new. He killed the centipede.

In telling himself it is only an element, nearly forgotten, of his memory—it is no longer tangible, no longer actual—he also convinces himself that this element of his youth was due to his stupidity. He never really knew just when and when not to make a stand.

The past never was. It's an easy answer, but a less painful one.

He turns off his oscilloscope and then, almost simultaneously, the dual pulsating lights. The music he leaves on. He closes his eyes to listen carefully to the lyrics of the song.

⁂

The lonesome spaceship moves steadily at .9 of c towards its destination. It will soon be swallowed, engulfed by the depth that surrounds it.

No one is aboard. That doesn't matter to the spaceship. It knows it must go on... Millions of fathoms beneath the surface of space lurk the million-year centipedes—the only creatures knowing why and how.

Wakelin follows the spaceship's progress—its destination is his destiny. He must catch up with it before it submerges. This is his immediate purpose.

⁂

He knows what is to come—he has been shown. He must make preparations.

He has no reason to open his eyes. The song tells him to beware the centipede that comes to crawl over his flesh, beware the death. He understands. Once had been the time when he sang and played guitar with what was known as an underground rock band in the late 1960's. That was long ago. The lyrics were his. He lived them.

It was said he had died. Perhaps. More likely, he thinks, he merely retreated within himself in disappearance. Drugs had something to do with it. Primarily, however, it was his dissatisfaction with humanity, *his* humanity. Everywhere he went anything he found was not good, not *right*. He strove for emotional, mental, personal perfection.

Eventually he began to look within. He had spent fruitless years, yet still he searched and yearned for that perfect Within. And now his time was nearly over. The time had come for the ultimate submergence into a space wherefrom no return was possible.

Death, sanity: the risks were great. The promise of fulfillment, of love and perfection, was even greater.

And meanwhile there was pain. Fear.

Greet the supraconscious, seeker. Greet the blood-stained hand that bids welcome to levels beneath your own. Enter not in fear, but in terror, for herein lies the secret which calls insanity home. Enter cautiously. Enter consciously, and you will perish in self. Abandon that which you've known, and enter anew and cleansed. Be purged of your uncleanliness by that entity that dwells in the deepest depth of infinite space. Enter, and be wary. Distortion lights the way.

Beware the centipede that comes to crawl over your flesh. Beware the death.

Wakelin, preoccupied with his thoughts, hardly noticed as he dressed to leave his room what he had chosen to wear. He gazed warily at his mirror. He had chosen a gray tweed three-piece suit, a white shirt with French cuffs, and red tennis shoes. Smiling, he left his room, locked the door, and caught an elevator just as it was closing. *Someone must have just gotten off,* he thought, for the elevator was empty. He rode the elevator non-stop from the fortieth floor on which he lived to the twenty-seventh, to the residence of one of his few acquaintances, the only one whom he knew from his days with The Hinge.

An attractive dark-haired girl wearing a leopard-skin answered the door.

"Oh, hi, Wakelin. How are you?"

Wakelin didn't answer. He stared at her hands. They were covered with blood.

"I'm sorry. I was just cutting some steaks for dinner—want to stay and eat with me?"

"Huh? Oh. Sure." Wakelin awkwardly entered the room, trying to avoid the blood-stained patches of floor. He found this increasingly hard to do as he neared the living-room. "Spilled a lot, didn't you?"

"Couple of drops, why? They're barely noticeable."

Wakelin waded ankle-deep through the living-room into the kitchen. He stopped moving. He stopped breathing. There, in the kitchen, lay a human corpse bleeding profusely. He waited. He couldn't move—paralyzed. Soon the blood reached up to his knee. The whole apartment was flooding. Still he remained indecisive, unsure as to how or why a body could bleed so much. Waste-deep he came to a decision. "Come on, let's get out of here before we drown."

"What are you talking about?"

"Come on. Hurry."

"Huh?"

"The blood. Now, come on."

"What blood? Those couple of drops? For chrissake, I'll shampoo the carpet later, okay?"

"We're going to drown—it's not slacking off."

"Aren't you funny. Ha ha."

Wakelin started to pull her out of the kitchen, trying to force her out of the apartment. She freed herself from his grip and almost immediately was submerged in the blood. She was a good deal shorter than Wakelin and was lost in the flood. Blindly and unsuccessfully, Wakelin tried to find her in the dark opaque liquid. Groping wildly until he was himself almost covered over, he eventually found the door to the apartment. He tumbled into the hallway, strangely alone. The blood remained in the apartment. He looked down at himself. No trace of blood remained on either him or his clothing.

Solemn and confused, he returned to his own apartment, locking the door behind himself and mourning the death of the girl he loved. He returned to his mirror and saw the tear-stained face with its blood-stained emotion.

chapter three

THE SPACESHIP CIRCLES DETERMINEDLY. The circles tighten increasingly toward the gap through which the ship will descend to the depth of the centipede. Soon the time will arrive.

Wakelin feels his nerves taking off in directions which he prefers they'd stay away from. In order to subdue the rampancy, he lights a joint and inhales the sweet-tasting smoke. It is good, but he has built up such a tolerance that one joint does little more than calm him a bit. He lights another. He sits deep in the plush armchair he doesn't own, listening to faint reverberations of what once was music. Lighting a third joint, he realizes that perhaps this is important—that reverberations underlie the very essence of music. A universal reverberation which underlies a universal musical essence awaits comprehension by mankind.

The spaceship has descended to the first level below that of consciousness, below thought, below music. Wakelin has followed.

Here is universal reverberation.

Here are the moments of birth and death; here is the level of insanity and blind faith; here is the level of emotion—naked and raw. Here is existence without thought.

All is mere pulsation. Red pulsations of pain. Blue pulsations of tranquility.

Almost like oceans, he sees them and avoids collision for the time being. He is aboard the spaceship and controls it.

The Sea of Joy, pulsating seemingly expandingly.

The Sea of Hope, pulsating like some long-forgotten refuge in the damp darkness of a Spanish galleon.

The Sea of Forgiveness, pulsating in direct opposition to the Sea of Vindictiveness.

Wakelin studies these carefully—wanting to learn what he can. But then, in the blackness of the space between the seas, he discovers a pulsation darker and more mysterious than the deepest space. A darkness of such kind as he would never have believed possible. Set apart from the rest, its pulsations are an incarnate act of swallowing, or engulfing. Wakelin sees this and understands that he must follow its beckoning. But not yet. He isn't fully prepared to enter the void of darkness. Further preparations have to be made. He shuts down the spaceship and, leaving it, decides to resurface one last time before entering that darkest doorway of pulsations that is the Sea of Death.

☢

Depth growing into brilliance—mind-shattering eye-burning illumination—light—nova—*purity* dawn

awakening

              cleansed

Sensation: cleansed

Sensation: growth

    Growing larger

    Growing conscious

              Pure Dawn.

⁂

The song has ended. Slowly Wakelin opens his eyes—absorbing his surroundings warily. He half expects them to take life and attack him.

They do not.

He wonders why he painted his walls a dark red. He wishes them black. He studies the overhead lights with suspicion. For the first time in months he turns them off. He fears them—they live.

He prepares himself.

⁂

The myriad lights pulsated wildly to the music—combining, forming, and disorganizing themselves again. Enchantedly, they engrossed themselves in the living thought of one man—the music and lyrics of Wakelin. Alone he stood at the helm, forefronting his keyboardist and his drummer. Alone he stood entranced yet driving onwards, enthralledly spewing forth flames of knowledge, touching those who drew too near, who saw too clearly the truth the man professed. He spoke with two voices as one—the deep, pain-striken mature voice of a genius and the wild furor of a madman. His throat and hands combined, bringing forth such sounds from vocal chords and guitar strings as few could ever describe. Teacher and savior, he told his tale once more:

In my mind the centipede crawls and dwells alone, aloof, lashing vehemently with tongue and fang. He buries to withdraw from you the remnants of some long-forgotten tribe—he is unalive—

Beware the centipede that comes to crawl over your flesh.

Beware the death.

chapter four

SOMEWHERE, A LONE BIRD soared through clouds, dipping, rolling, and rising again playfully. Below, he saw the power inherent in motion, he saw a train hurriedly passing through his green land. He gracefully dropped to within fifteen yards of the turbulent creation. He was confident his time had come to surpass it. As if the essence of love, he flew faster than the very mechanical thought expanded its reality into his. He was its god. He was its love.

Elsewhere, an innocent was seduced to the ways of joy—imperfection. Hardly a perfectionist, he noticed only peripherally what was happening. The transfer of religion frightened him little—he worshipped a man who had played guitar. A board of cork hung on a wall in a room. Upon it a darkened picture of a man with his truest love, a microphone, was centered in among martyr-images and crucifixes. This was what it had all ended in—shades of dark, shadows of death. The innocent smiled sardonically.

Choking, coughing, spluttering, yet not realizing, a blindman dies a silent death in a barren cubicle, strangely drowning in an unseen blood. He will never understand. It is nothing new—only now it is growing into universal proportions. Trial by death.

Everywhere, blindmen mechanically propelling themselves through space and time, running into walls, into each other, into death. This is the truth behind life. Wakelin sees. Wakelin knows.

But he had tried to warn them all. However, they were blind.

Between your legs, between your dreams, he comes to slither past unseen, to leave his imprint on your soul, and bludgeon-feast from parts a whole. A creature knows creation-self and death beneath him's unimport, Just wary be of sanity, for it is mere illusory and spews on winds as sand-cast fort.

Beware the centipede that comes to crawl over your flesh. Beware the death.

He loved. He had loved fervently, believingly. His love manifested itself in death. Because he loved, death embraced his life and the two became as one: a monism built in an effort to please liquid structures, built upon the shedding of blood.

chapter five

CIRCLE

expansion

equilibrial definity

Saffron

Saffron

life is made

of

is of

Circle.

Swirling clouds of death penetrate the soul of a life-lorn love-torn strife, amid protuberances of hope and minimal existence.

Have you ever seen a centipede flattened against the wall? If you ever see a centipede, you'll see no one at all; they crawl across your mind at night and take the parts that are sane. Have you ever seen a centipede flattened against your brain? Once I was a small believer telling everybody else's pain. Now I know

I'm ill with fever; now I know I've gone insane. Won't it please destroy your fate; won't it please stand still? Have you ever seen a centipede flattened against your will?

⁂

The time has come. As somewhere two globules of darkness in a field of two-dimension run parallel until passing into dimensions apart from one another, a man must pass even further into unknown dimensions, even beneath the first layer which lies below; pulsation.

Wakelin sees. Wakelin knows. He must follow the path which has beckoned him to follow—into the dimensions within the engulfing Sea of Death.

He travels—alone in his ship he traverses the remaining space until he enters the void of pure darkness.

All is still.

chapter six

DETERMINE
  Earth
    Atrophy
    Thorough
                De-Ea-At-Th
                Death
                EAT(
sustenance is found here)
substance is found here.
                Do not complain.
all you need   is here.
all you bleed
all your speed
all you've freed
all you breed
all your creed
all you seed

all your deed

    deed

    deaddeaddeaddead.

          (dead)

QUESTION: WHAT IS ALL YOU NEED?

WAKELIN: SANITY; LOVE.

QUESTION: WHICH?

WAKELN: THEY ARE SYNONYMOUS.

QUESTION: WHAT IS ALL YOU BLEED?

WAKELIN: ALL I LOVE.

QUESTION: YOU NEED LOVE YET YOUR LOVE KILLS?

WAKELIN: YES.

QUESTION: WHAT IS ALL YOUR SPEED?

WAKELIN: THE HINGE.

QUESTION: YOUR PAST?

WAKELIN: MY PAST. PERHAPS IT NEVER WAS.

QUESTION: I DON'T UNDERSTAND.

WAKELIN: IT'S AN EASY ANSWER, BUT LESS PAINFUL.

QUESTION: WHAT IS ALL YOU'VE FREED?

WAKELIN : ALL I LOVE.

QUESTION: FREED FROM WHAT?

WAKELIN : ME; LIFE.

QUESTION: ARE THEY SYNONYMOUS?

WAKELIN: NO.

QUESTION: WHAT IS ALL YOU BREED?

 WAKELIN: PAIN.

QUESTION: FOR YOURSELF?

WAKELIN: YES.

QUESTION: WHAT IS ALL YOUR CREED?

WAKELIN : INTENSITY.

QUESTION: WHY?

WAKELIN: TO LEARN. ALL PEOPLE BY NATURE DESIRE TO KNOW.

QUESTION: THE NUMBER OF TRUE PEOPLE AMONG YOUR KIND IS SMALL.

WAKELIN: YES—THE INFLUX OF MACHINERY IN THE...

QUESTION: WHAT IS ALL YOU SEED?

WAKELIN: DISCONTENT WITH MINIMAL EXISTENCE.

QUESTION: HOW?

WAKELIN: BY FINDING VALUE IN INTENSITY.

QUESTION: EVEN PAIN?

WAKELIN: YES.

QUESTION: AND LOVE?

WAKELIN: YES.

QUESTION: AND SANITY? OR INSANITY?

WAKELIN: YES, BOTH. IN EVERYTHING.

QUESTION: YET YOU LACK LOVE AND SANITY, OR PROPER INTENSITY THEREOF?

WAKELIN: PROPER INTENSITY THEREOF.

QUESTION: WHAT IS ALL YOUR DEED?

WAKELIN: LIFE.

QUESTION: WHAT WAS ITS VALUE?

WAKELIN: I LEARNED, BUT NOT ENOUGH.

QUESTION: DID YOU FIND PROPER INTENSITY IN LIFE?

WAKELIN: I FOUND PROXIMITY TO DEATH.

QUESTION: YOU DESIRE THE INTENSITY OF DEATH?

WAKELIN: YES.

QUESTION: PROCEED THEN. deaddeaddeaddead.

chapter seven

THE BLACKNESS PROCESSES ITS void in correspondence with red pulsations, and amid it all Wakelin sees.

At first an outline, vague and detached from his depth, pervades the pulse. Wakelin nears it, yet doesn't move—his world contracts.

He recognizes a human figure, realizes her color hair, her color eyes, her scantily-clad bodily persistence.

"Hello, Dot," he speaks, in a tone so low he afterwards feels self-assured of its inaudibility. Somewhat louder, he adds, "I'm confused."

"Wakelin. Take me home. I don't like this."

"Sure. What don't you like?"

The girl named Dot hesitates noticeably. "Your love is different."

Wakelin falls silent.

☢

"I hate that tree."

Wakelin stares out of his parked car at a peculiar death of perversion—a smallish former tree mocking the trees that half-encircle it. It defies the sun and rejects erectness—it has developed into an angular misshapen ridicule perpetuating its compromise between soil and heavens, suspended at an angle perpendicular to neither.

He speaks to his lover, who sits across the confines of his car, struggling to see some rational element in what Wakelin says. But Wakelin sees, Wakelin knows.

He claims that such a tree is a sham of reality—an entity devoid of all right to existence, which resultingly should be condemned to a non-reality, or a different one.

What his lover saw in him she said frightened her. But it was too late. She had already told him that the night before that they had spent together was all there ever could be between them—that it had been special but she couldn't handle it. She was grateful but terrified.

Wakelin saw and understood.

⁂

Wakelin sees the girl named Dot. She hadn't been the girl by the tree.

Yet his world continues to contract, so much so that for him only two realities exist—himself and other. That, just as the other consists of a myriad of images—the tree and its girl, the girl named Dot, the Hinge—so too a multitude of suppurations and sustenances comprise his self.

He pauses. Wakelin no longer sees anything. All has reverted to a dark emphasis which he can only sense internally—the darkness of truth. He attempts to conjure up an image in his mind but even the vision of his memory is denied him.

He is totally alone in his own self. He knows he has lost all other.

Finding nothing particularly peculiar in this, he resigns himself to the culmination of his directive.

chapter Eight

THE INNOCENT WORSHIPPED A man who had played guitar. On the second of July 1978, he made the sojourn to Los Angeles to find the man named Wakelin, who had disappeared one day short of seven years before.

He checked into the Wakelin Hotel in the evening. Here, he thought, was as good a place as any to look——the Hinge had released an album many years ago which pictured this hotel on its cover.

The area seems a rather unpleasant one——but he is here, safe in his room. Perhaps. As he reads what he finds written on the wall he begins to wonder.

⁂

Laura became crazy very crazy
and stayed because Ceasar
would only come out at night.
Ceasar didn't become crazy he became
the devil man who only came
out at night to kill his wife her

name was Laura R.
But at last they both
stayed together for
ever.
I was the only witness to
all of this thing that happened
here in this room.
Two people died here
because of the boogey-
man and they died because
nobody said nothing to them.
close your window
and door
so that the
boogey-man won't get you
when you're alone
at night.
Good
luck
to
those who
stay here in
his room.

❖

The innocent does not yet bother to unpack his one bag and its scanty contents of clothing, music, and a couple of books. He lies down on his bed, faces the ceiling, and smokes a cigarette as he stares at the patterns formed by cracks. He dreams of meeting Wakelin and following him to the truth. He is fearful of failure, needing a way to work it out should his dream fall through. A poet, the innocent decides to sketch an account of the weekend as it passes.

☢

Nine o'clock. Dark outside. Inside one faint overhead light and three empty light sockets. One outlet in the bathroom with my cassette machine playing every Hinge Wakelin vocals song released.

Outside the hotel, before I checked in, a woman wearing dark glasses, looking very much like a prostitute, started talking, seemingly at me—but no it was only to herself.

Checked in—Rm. 222—$14 for two nights. I don't have a key. The desk clerk unlocks for me when I return—he seems to be all right.

Told him someone might come to meet me—a man in his thirties named Wakelin. He suggested I leave a message. Did:

Wakelin—

Ray told me you were alive and would meet me here. If so, I'm in room 222.

Jim.

Went to my room. Remembered that I was supposed to send postcard to this fantastic musician friend I'm falling for. Went downstairs, not locking door—thought I need key to—told man behind desk I had to go out, would he lock my door?

He said he found a reasonable tissuesque substitution for lack of toilet-paper in my bathroom. I said good, no great, could he put it in my room when he went up to lock my room's door. You didn't lock it? No, do they lock without a key. They're supposed to. Sorry.

Asked him where I could go to buy stamps—tells me a million places I haven't faintest idea of locations of. I go outside, getting dark—I don't want to be out at night alone in this part of town. Walk up Hope to Hyatt Regency—buy card and stamps. Walk back—ask to be let in room—write card, start this, now wondering why I don't have a key and the writing on the wall.

Now wondering if I should sleep. Yes.

Wakelin has been messianic for me for quite a long while. This is the culmination of years of dreaming.

A while back I heard an interview with Ray Douer, the Hinge's keyboardist. Five, six years ago. Maybe less. I don't really remember when. He said Wakelin was always fascinated with the image of a shooting star—something that appears out of nowhere, is spectacular and fantastic, and then as quickly as it appeared disappears again. This was me, I thought.

Bought their album *Los Angeles* sometime a couple of years ago—during my sentence served at Northwestern University—loneliness—lyrics, Wakelin's, described me.

Went to Lake Forest College. Bought *Waking in the Blood*, with lyrics to "The Million-Year Centipede" included. Before this, I heard Douer again, claiming Wakelin may have faked his own death—the circumstances were strange. The body that was supposedly his had the internal organs of a 65-year-old man.

"Centipede" said: Three years shy of a decade I was forced to be away—an exile from the land of strength and sagacity and justice.

Now I have returned, my friends. Sleep now, for tomorrow you must follow as I retrace my lonesome steps. Prepare yourselves.

Seven years after his supposed death was July 3, 1978. Seven years of exile. The land of strength and sagacity and justice? He disappeared in Paris, but lived in L.A.

A vision came to me—Wakelin facing west, L.A. I had had, according to my roommate, at least one conversation with Wakelin in my sleep, so a vision didn't really surprise me.

Sometimes I've taken this "mission" very seriously, other times I doubted its validity. At least two relationships were ended as a result of my beliefs. I was fired from my job for the same—without ever forcing my belief on anyone. They asked—I explained.

I shall soon know.

But now, when I go home and show this to my musician friend Tricia, can she accept this? Or will she also be afraid of me and retreat?

Please, Tricia, see how important this was for me, and do not reject me for it. I am very worried by this—by you. You don't know how much I enjoy you and how much I want something like this not to come between us. It's your sensitivity I first found most enticing—so be sensitive, as I know you can, to my peculiarity, to this which had to be, regardless.

☙

Almost noon—waking in the blood. Woke up 10:30—washed up—and went for food. New desk clerk—older than the other. Told him I was leaving. Went to a place called Armanayda. A coffee shop where I had coffee, Coke, and a double cheeseburger and bought a pack of cigarettes all for less than $3. Came back and checked for messages from Wakelin—none—and told clerk my message was there for a 34-year-old man I'm supposed to meet.

Listening now to "What Saved You"—a very fine Wakelin tune from *Worthy Dreams Without a Mind*. My 6' x 3' silkscreen Wakelin poster hangs on the curtain—his book *The Butterfly Catchers and The Centipedes* sits on a table, along with *The Encyclopedia of Rock* opened to the Hinge page history of Wakelin. Five pictures balanced on the table lean against the wall. My tapes. On the nightstand my airplane ticket, my map of L.A., cards, my latest book of poems, two pens, three Michael Moorcock books (the man whose novel *Black Corridor* in summer '75 changed my state from blissful ignorance to painful comprehension—saw the light).

On other table my washstuff, cigs & matches, my bag with dirty clothes. Hole in wall behind headboard of bed (two shelves) holds jacket on one, clean clothes on lower. Bed has U.S. Army blanket—unmade (thank god—I don't want anyone coming in here when I'm not here). In my hand a pen, a stack of paper atop my closed notebook *unterlage* in which my novel, your poem, Tricia, and your phone & address, my poem for class, and the poems of my classmates are.

On first table also sits a note I wrote on the plane for my postcard to my special musician friend: yodel apple strudel, thrash and throttle poodle. Makes no sense I know, but that's what I wrote.

Already mailed card on way to Armanayda. Will be there probably 5th, maybe 6th.

☢

The room:

Sitting on the bed looking toward the bathroom.

The chair sits a foot and a half from the bed. In terms of my boots (10½'s), the room measures 14¾ bootlengths x 12 boot-lengths. The bathroom 5¾ x 3. The room isn't too small, nor really bad. I'm beginning to feel comfortable here. Day throws a new perspective on everything. The area seems better—I feel less nervous about the whole thing—the whole trip.

This is the best part of the trip—the best part.

I'm beginning to think what to do for dinner. I think I'll splurge (I've $34 left) and go to the Hyatt Regency. The time is now 1:15.

3:00. Read a little Moorcock—Wakelin music non-stop. Just finished some solitaire. My best friend Ernie phoned me. I was lying on my bed, and someone assertively knocked on my door. My heart jumped. It was the clerk telling me I had a call. Went downstairs and talked for a while with Ernie. He told the clerk he was my lawyer and that the extradition charges had been dropped and that he had to talk to me. I played it up on the phone—the clerk was only six feet away. Hearing from Ernie was good—very good. The clerk let me back in my room.

Before, sometime, a Spanish or Asian guy (I didn't get a good look at him) wanted to check into the hotel while I was downstairs. The clerk looked—he had no room except one without a bath for $6. The guy said he'd be back later to see if the situation had changed. There are plenty of hotels in this area—why was he apparently so set on the Wakelin? Could it be that he too is looking for Wakelin? I wouldn't be surprised—I can't be the only person who'd thought to find him here now. Some sort of logic is behind this.

Tonight will answer me one way or another.

If I find Wakelin I have to follow him—I may not return, in which case no one will be able to read this.

This is so damn important to me it's freaking the living crap out of me. A mind-trip.

All through the day—I me mind, I me mind.

Read more Moorcock. I noticed the time was passing quickly—it was almost seven. I decided I'd better eat—wasn't feeling too well. Maybe hunger. Went, as decided, to Hyatt Regency to the coffee shop for a Reuben and Heineken's. Had a thirst for a good beer. Walked back but still felt ill—I felt a headache coming on though my stomach was settled. Waited for 45 minutes for the clerk to show up to let me into my room. An old man waited an hour—he needed a room. He talked a bit—he had hopped a freight from Colorado. He had been in a war. I couldn't catch most of this due to his speech difficulty he was old and rather shaky and could barely speak understandably. He talked about being on a ship and how one guy had shot another over a crap game. And about guns—lots about guns—a Thompson, a 45, and, believe it, a bazooka! He talked more. Where could he buy a comb and tennis shoes. Where are oranges around here from. I told him Napa—I didn't know. He asked me where I worked—told him I didn't—that I was unemployed. Where your money from? Saved up from when working—had some left. Where'll you get money? Unemployment. Oh, after oranges, I told him Napa was nice—a lot of wine grown there. He said he couldn't see drinking wine—in this heat beer was best, cold beer. I said it's good, but so's cold wine. But winter Tequila, I rather unemotionally postulated. He said more—most of which I missed, the rest ambiguously unimportant. The clerk came, showed me to my room, and later came back and brought me a clean towel (he had supplied me with an ancient bar of soap and a slightly used towel yesterday).

I felt good to be back in my room—like being home. I'm getting used to these people— they're really fairly nice. One said hello to me as I left for dinner as he sat on the entrance drinking some wine; another when I waited for the clerk offered me a drink of bourbon which I refused—wish I hadn't—I did because he offered it to the old man too and he had turned it down—I like keeping patterns sometimes. Another guy in a Chinese or Japanese shirt and pants (he, as most here, looked down and out) came down also as I waited for the clerk. Asked me to stop at his room on 2nd floor—first atop the stairs—when the clerk came back and to let him know. I didn't want to but said sure but felt much better when he came back down almost simultaneously with the return of the clerk, so he saved me the trouble. He also had a star-earring in his left ear. This afternoon a dog was barking a lot—it's yelping right now. I met—no, I saw, not met—several other people who also live here—another old man almost rickety as the one from Colorado. Another guy with a minuscule beard (in anticipation of goatee). A family who all were fat and the lady of which always says hi when she sees me or anyone else. Hi guys—to me and the old Coloradan.

Everything's all right here. Nobody bothers anyone without provocation. So long as I don't provoke anyone I'm all right, even in their eyes, I suspect. A very large anonymous family precariously but mutually-respectingly built.

⁂

Eight o'clock. I may be hearing things.

Thought I heard a conversation upstairs—someone telling someone else in a deep resonant voice that he was Wakelin—the second scoffing unbelievingly, sarcastically saying you're Wakelin, huh.

I've turned up my Hinge tapes louder—I can't hear the conversation anymore, but maybe if that is Wakelin he'll hear the music and will know I'm here.

⁂

11:30 almost—read in Moorcock and the *Rock Encyclopedia*. Midnight I went to sleep and figured if anything happened, it'd have to wake me up, or else when I did go to sleep I'd never be up in time to make my noon flight. I had time to smoke a cigarette, undress, and prepare for bed. I was very tired.

Am I too much into my own thing? Will Tricia think so? I've always really basically been a loner of sorts.

The stomach pain is back.

chapter NINE

WAKELIN'S BASEMENT FELL SILENT. There he and a friend, also a guitarist, would jam together for hours.

Wakelin's health was ebbing. During the last lengthy jam, on an old blues riff, he'd had several coughing fits. He merely stopped playing, reached for his bottle of tequila, poured himself a shot, and held it in his hand. He stared at it. He found he was incapable of holding it steady—it shivered as Wakelin's whole body shivered.

It entranced Wakelin.

His friend stopped playing. Nothing was said.

Wakelin sees this as clearly as he ever had. It had been the first incident in his life which had told him that it would be possible for his death to come in some way other than conscious suicide.

Why should he see this—only this?

He tries to concentrate on prior and after. What had happened before this incident and what had followed it both elude him.

Soon his thoughts on this jam also dissipate. Again he is totally alone. Nothing else exists.

He is the universe.

When he has come to this revelation, a torrent of images—some distant, some foreign, some within himself—takes control of the ether which now seemingly contains his universe, his self.

Out of the darkness, a faint point of scarlet is visible. Its hue varies perceptibly as it nears Wakelin. Crimson. Rust. Maroon. Magenta.

The point grows, no longer from the ether but from Wakelin's self.

Ruby. Carmine.

It fills all that is Wakelin.

Blood.

Faces appear in the ether. The confused expression of a girl who had drowned in her apartment and Wakelin had been unable to save. A blindman who had been a close friend, sardonically content. The dispassionate stern frowns of his parents, whom he claimed dead long before they ever were. The Hinge, the ragged and beaten yet still fiery eyes of a keyboardist who tried to see and could not and a drummer whose fear of Wakelin's image forbade him all seeing. The mournful tear-streaked faces of a hundred lovers he'd had, all traces of self-piety scourged from their souls. Wakelin smiles at them—he had always said it would come to this. An army of thousands upon thousands of unfamiliar faces—old, young, male, female—all with closed eyes and blank expressions. Fools and blindmen.

The images fade. Color retreats into the ether. Again Wakelin is alone.

He begins to remember, as if being fed vignettes of his life.

chapter ten

QUESTION: WHAT IS ALL YOU NEED?
WAKELIN: SANITY; LOVE.
QUESTION: WHICH?
WAKELIIN: THEY ARE SYNONYMOUS.

❖

A rapid succession of attempted telephone calls is unsuccessful. Midnight is long past. Wakelin sits on his bed in his small dormitory room. He has turned out all the lights except the flare of a saffron candle, which declares its potency, standing on the floor before his feet. Again he reaches alongside the candle for the phone, which holds a greater passion. He redials the same number. The line remains busy. He has been trying to call one girl for over an hour. He dials the number again a minute later. Still busy.

He is angry. He needs to talk with her for he feels depressed. Their relationship hasn't been progressing recently.

He has had much to drink. He stares another bottle of inexpensive red wine—a California Pedroncelli—into submission. He grips it one-handed around its neck with the force of surrogation. He pulls it from the floor violently and lifts it to his mouth. He swallows a great deal of it, so quickly that he coughs some and his eyes water a little.

Then his eyes fill with tears and he begins muttering self-pity to himself. Anger replaces this soon. He picks up the phone and tries again, unsuccessfully.

He has an idea. He gets up from the bed, crosses the room, reaches the light-switch, and turns on the overhead lamp. He returns across the room, kneels at the foot of his bed, and pulls out from underneath it a small cardboard box filled with matchbooks. He places the box on a small bar-table that stands in the center of the room. On it rests an old ceramic ashtray.

Wakelin walks around to his desk and finds his Swiss Army knife. He folds open the longest blade and walks back again to the bar-table. He opens the cardboard box and pulls out a matchbook. He uncovers it and cuts off the heads of all of the matches. These he tosses into the ashtray. He keeps doing this until the ashtray is half-filled with matchheads.

Wakelin returns to his desk and, from another ashtray, skewers with the point of his knife-blade three centipedes which he has crushed over the last few days. These he carries over to the bar-table and distributes over the half-filled ceramic ashtray. He turns off the light, extinguishes the candle, and strikes a match. He places the ashtray on the floor next to the phone and drops the lit match into it.

The flame surges explosively. Wakelin stares at the pyre, intent upon his worship of death. He chants the Hare Krishna mantra he had once been taught without comprehending why. This is as everything in his universe should be, he concludes. The flame begins to falter as the pyre spews forth the knowledge inherent in smoke.

Wakelin's eyes water violently, but he notices neither the smoke nor his own emotion. He becomes the dying flame, the glowing embers, the consumed bodies of three centipedes.

He watches voyeuristically until nothing remains. After a lengthy silence, a complete death of all rational thought and sensory perception, he picks up the phone in the darkness.

He dials carefully. Still the line is busy.

Wakelin screams, throws the phone across the room, jumps up, hurries to his desk, finds his keys, and runs out of the room. He runs down the hall, out the door, and heads for his car. He is determined to find the girl.

☢

Wakelin makes the forty-minute drive from his present school to his former school, where the girl, named Janet, lives and studies, in twenty minutes.

They had met at a party for freshman journalism majors on the first day of classes the previous year. Wakelin remembers first seeing her there. He had thought he'd make love to her that night. She'd asked him to walk her home, and he'd been certain.

Here he was—a year and several months later—still a virgin. Their friendship reminded him constantly that he was a confirmed masochist. He was also enough of a sadist to retaliate.

He turns on the hardest rock and roll he can find on his car radio, opened all his windows, and screames vague lyrics—his own substitution for the actual—driving hatefully toward an uncertain destination.

⚛

Wakelin leaps from his car up the stairs of the women's dormitory where Janet lives. He pulls open the door so forcefully it cracks against its stop. He directs himself menacingly to the dorm phone, picks it up, and in his haste misdials. He tries again. Janet's roommate answers, noticeably annoyed at the interruption. She tells him Janet is at the library. Wakelin thinks a moment whether to believe her or not. He decides he has to, for he knows no way past the security system to check for himself. He lights a cigarette and walks slowly to the library, trying to collect himself.

The man at the entrance desk refuses him entrance to the library. Wakelin says he has an emergency, that his father is on faculty and has asked him to get a book for some crucial research project. The man refuses admittance. Wakelin does not have a current ID card for the school.

Why the fuck did I ever go to school here, Wakelin thinks as he curses his way outside again. Depressed, he goes to find his car. All he can think of is to return to his room and drink.

chapter eleven

QUESTION: WHAT IS ALL YOU BLEED?
WAKELIN: ALL I LOVE.
QUESTION: YOU NEED LOVE, YET YOUR LOVE KILLS?
WAKELIN: YES.

Wakelin stands before his mirror wondering how he had done it. He had loved the girl for years and now she was dead. He had killed her. She had been drowned in someone else's blood. Perhaps it had been Wakelin's own blood.

She hadn't been the first, either. Hundreds had perished. Fifteen thousand. Anything, any part of Wakelin's memory and dreams was destined for this death.

Wakelin weeps as he stands before his mirror, unable to see it anymore. He falls to the floor.

"God, this is fucked! Let me kill myself—let me die!"

He screams until he passes out.

Wakelin needs to talk with Janet, for he feels depressed. He has been drinking very heavily. Alone. He feels more alone than he ever has. Or maybe more depressed. Or more drunk.

He phones Janet, straining to be intelligible. She tells him she's very busy studying. He slurs a proclamation of love over and over. She tells him she has no time right now and hangs up the phone.

Wakelin smiles. His thoughts tremble. He goes into his dresser, fumbling for an old aspirin bottle. He finds it, scrutinizes it, and opens it. He shakes the contents into his hand. His hand shakes as he brings it to his mouth. He swallows the twenty sleeping pills that he had been keeping in the bottle. He had bought them the previous week on the morning after he had slit his left wrist with his Swiss Army knife. He had known this would happen.

He redials Janet's phone number. "Hello?"

"Hi."

"Wakelin, I don't have time..."

"Listen to me Janet. Do me a favor?"

"What?"

"Make sure—will you take care of my poetry?"

"What? What do you mean."

"Promise me you'll take care of my poetry."

"What are you talking about? What's going on?"

"Going on? Nothing. My poetry... Will you? Promise."

"You're not making any sense."

"I love you Janet." Wakelin pauses.

"You're not making sense—what's the matter?"

"Promise me you'll take care of my poetry. I've just taken

twenty sleeping pills."

"What?"

"Take care of my poetry."

chapter twelve

QUESTION: WHAT IS ALL YOUR SPEED?

WAKELIN : THE HINGE.

QUESTION: YOUR PAST?

WAKELIN: MY PAST. PERHAPS IT NEVER WAS.

QUESTION: I DON'T UNDERSTAND.

WAKELIN: IT'S AN EASY ANSWER, BUT LESS PAINFUL.

"Where the hell have you been? We ran through the sound-check hours ago."

Wakelin shrugs in answer as he walks past the annoyance provided by the concert-hall stage-hand. He opens the door to his dressing-room. Ray Douer is sitting on a butterfly-chair, talking to two overly mascara'd, overly buxom young girls who sit at his feet on the floor. They both stand when they see Wakelin enter the room. Ray, however, pays little attention and continues the story he is telling.

Wakelin walks to his dressing-table and pours himself a shot of tequila. He downs it immediately with the grace of a serpent slithering through slime. He lights up an opiated joint and inhales the smoke deeply. He hands the joint to one of the girls.

The girls talk to Wakelin. Ray continues his story. Wakelin hears nothing but the cacophony of further annoyance. A small speaker in the ceiling monitors the music that is being played for the waiting audience. The concert is scheduled to begin in a half-hour. Wakelin's attention focuses on this music. He listens to the guitar. He feels it encircle his head, going around and around. He sits down in another butterfly-chair and feels it spinning even more vehemently.

Wakelin closes his eyes. Somebody nudges him in the arm. He looks up to see his joint returned to him. He takes it and lowers it to the crotch of his black vinyl pants, burning end outwards. He stares at the smoke that curls up from it. It begins to from patterns in time to the music. Wakelin smiles at this observation, brings the joint back up and draws on it deeply again. He passes it to one of the girls again.

He looks up at Ray. He stares at Ray's narrow features. He wonders at Ray's gold-rim eyeglasses. He starts to say something but thinks the better of it and remains silent.

Wakelin smiles at a private thought. He begins to quote a theatrical piece he had written:

"Three years shy of a decade I was forced to be away—an exile from the land of strength and sagacity and justice. Now I have returned, my friends. Sleep now, for tomorrow you must follow as I retrace my lonesome steps. Prepare yourselves."

The stage manager enters the room and tells Wakelin and Ray that it is time. Wakelin smiles again, sardonically.

"For my death, friends," he half-whispers. He stands up and leaves the room, followed by Ray and the stage manager.

The drummer finds Ray and Wakelin, and the three walk on stage.

Wakelin straps on his Telecaster and walks to the microphone.

"Hello, Miami. Are you having fun this evening?"

The crowd cheers.

The cheers neither relent nor abate. The concert per se is ended, and the crowd yells for more. Adhering to a nearly universal musical code of behavior, the audience uniformly strikes matches and lights lighters to signify its desire for encores. Obligatorily, the Hinge return to the stage.

The drummer strikes the beat, and Ray and Wakelin melodify one of the numerous pieces of nearly epic proportions in their repertoire. Wakelin half-sings, half-preaches his poetry. The band attains an instrumental middle-eight. Wakelin interrupts it by reclaiming his microphone.

"Want to see my cock?"

The crowd screams its approval.

Wakelin unstraps his guitar, unzips his black vinyl pants, pulls out his cock, and dances about the stage for a while, his cock revolving in time to the music provided by the drums and keyboards. He turns to his amplifier and enjoys a long piss aimed directly at it.

The lights of the recording studio further heat the bodies of the sweating musicians.

Wakelin had been invited to a jam session. He had accepted and shown up. Now he stands before his mic, unaccustomed to the instrument he has decided to play—the blues harp. He looks to his left and sees Jimi Hendrix and Johnny Winter, both playing their guitars. Behind the three are Noel Redding, Jimi's bassist, and a drummer.

Is this alcoholic disrepair?

Wakelin fights to retain his consciousness, fighting drunkenness and stupor. He himself barely hears the music, interspersing his harp whenever he remembers to.

"Peoples Peoples Peoples, you know what it means to be left alone..."

chapter Thirteen

QUESTION: WHAT IS ALL YOU'VE FREED?
WAKELIN: ALL I LOVE.
QUESTION: FREED FROM WHAT?
WAKELIN: ME; LIFE.
QUESTION: ARE THEY SYNONYMOUS?
WAKELIN: NO.

☢

The group pairs up for what its minister calls "the faithwalk." Each person is to lead his trusting blind-folded partner across varied terrain at the lakefront retreat center where Wakelin's high school church group has decided to spend the weekend.

A few of the pairs head for a small circle of boarded-up shacks. Wakelin's partner suggests the same. Wakelin agrees without hesitation. He decides that he would very much like to be high.

The half-dozen renegades enter the nearest openable shack. One removes a pipe from the pocket of his jacket. Another simultaneously removes a bag of dope from his. The one hands his pipe to the other, who fills it and lights it, inhaling the smoke and coughing as he tries to hold it in.

Wakelin eventually is handed the pipe. He inhales. He too coughs, but violently. His eyes water. The others chortle. Wakelin begins to feel ill. A cold sweat breaks out on his back and forehead. He becomes very dizzy.

"I don't feel too well," he proclaims, leaving accompanied by a sinister laughter.

He hastily walks to the cabin in which he is staying. Upon entering the front-door he finds the counselors discussing the upcoming activities with the minister.

The minister asks, "Aren't you supposed to be on your faith-walk?"

"I just came in to freshen up."

The adults laugh at his remark. Wakelin is upset at this but feels too poorly to complain. He rushes to the washroom and throws up until he dry-heaves. He washes up and goes to the room where he has unrolled his sleeping bag. He lies down upon it, wishing he were dead rather than in so much pain. He decides he is dying and feels some solace in this thought.

Wakelin rests undisturbed until a girl enters the room: Beth. Wakelin remembers that she had been missing with a friend of his named Art from a large group meeting the previous evening.

"What are you doing here, Beth? Aren't you supposed to be on your faith-walk?"

"I had a headache, so I came back for my pills."

"Oh God, I've got a really bad one too. Can you lend me a couple?"

"Sure. Just a second." She leaves the room but returns in a moment. "Here—I've taken mine. These are prescription—you can keep them."

"Thanks." Wakelin opens the bottle and shakes out two tablets, swallowing them without water.

"You feel bad?"

"Christ, I sure do."

"Would you like a back-rub?"

"What would Art think?"

"I'm not really his girlfriend." Beth sits down next to Wakelin, who is lying on his stomach. She begins to rub his back.

"That's good. Thanks Beth." He lets her continue. "I'm tired—I think I'll take a nap."

"Well, how about a good-night kiss?"

"Sure."

Beth nears Wakelin and they kiss long and deep. Her kiss hurts his lip as she probes his throat with her tongue. He finds the pain exciting and tells her she kisses well. He turns his head the other way to let her know he wants to sleep.

⁂

Early evening Wakelin wakes up again. It is supper time. Wakelin sits down with his paper-plate filled with hot dogs and baked beans. Beth walks over and sits next to him. She begins to question him about his feelings toward her. He tells her he likes her but enjoys not having a commitment to anyone and intends not to. She seems flummoxed but remains silent.

⁘

The evening's activities are interrupted for Wakelin when another girl disturbs his writing to tell him that Beth is in near-hysterics and says only that she wants to see him. Wakelin puts down his pen, closes his notebook, and with a curse leaves the room.

He finds Beth in front of the fireplace in the living-room, whimpering. He sits down next to her and puts his arm around her.

"Beth? What's wrong?"

She explains how she is unloved and how she wishes she and Wakelin could have a relationship and how she just wants to die. Wakelin is dumbstruck. He had been saying the same things for years and wondered why people backed away from him. He too had often been through near-suicidal hysteria. He feels so close to Beth it makes him very uncomfortable. She is invading his private hallowed domain of self-pity and pain. He tells her he cares for her but cannot have a relationship with anyone. It quiets her temporarily. He begins to tell her about his own pain, to console her. Before long she renews her crying.

Wakelin stands up and turns to another girl, the girl who had told him initially of Beth's condition.

"You talk to her—I can't handle it anymore."

Wakelin leaves the cabin and goes for a long walk by the lake.

chapter Fourteen

QUESTION: WHAT IS ALL YOU BREED?
WAKELIN: PAIN.
QUESTION: FOR YOURSELF?
WAKELIN: YES.

☢

A young Wakelin has finished second grade. His grammar school prepares for the field day that follows the last day of classes.

For the last year and a half Wakelin has had a girlfriend named Lee Anne. They have long prepared for eventual marriage—even deciding on names for their prospective children.

For Lee Anne and Wakelin it is their last summer together—he must move with his family elsewhere. They won't be able to share any more recesses. They won't kiss behind the school's playground bushes again.

Neither understands their bond, but both accept it.

Now Wakelin prepares for the fifty-yard dash he has been signed up for. He runs around and around the vast playground.

Lee Anne follows him.

Wakelin stops after a while—he sits down on the grass and starts to cry.

"What's wrong?" Lee Anne asks him.

"Leave me alone," Wakelin demands. "I just want to get ready for the race. Leave me alone."

Lee Anne leaves him alone. She too is crying, but honors his desire.

Wakelin cries even more. He cannot understand why.

The argument itself was of minimal importance.

Wakelin is running away. He follows the wooded mountain path far ahead of his family. He is angry and cannot retort. His arguments had hardly been heard.

He is very angry. He has run as quickly as possible to the small plateau which crests the Alberta mountain the family has meandered onto.

He realizes he has left everything well behind. He climbs onto a boulder that is embedded into the edge of the precipice. He overlooks the edge to see a straight drop onto a thick forest of firs and pines.

He stands there still, growing depressed in his anger and wondering if he jumped how much it would hurt. He pictures himself skewered by one of the distant firs.

Soon he realizes less fear. He begins to weep. He hasn't wept for many years but does so now, for he is alone and lonely for love.

The tears bring him courage, and he decides to jump. He leans over the edge precariously, staring intently below, trying to find a good target. He loses his balance but manages to straighten himself up once more.

He thinks he hears his family coming.

Wakelin goes to rejoin them.

chapter Fifteen

QUESTION: WHAT IS ALL YOUR CREED?

WAKELIN : INTENSITY.

QUESTION: WHY?

WAKELIN: TO LEARN. ALL PEOPLE BY NATURE DESIRE TO KNOW.

QUESTION: THE NUMBER OF TRUE PEOPLE AMONG YOUR KIND IS SMALL. WAKELIN: YES—THE INFLUX OF MACHINERY IN THE...

☢

WAKELIN: I thought it was a good film. I particularly thought the portrayal of the post-war psyche of an emotionally gun shot war veteran was excellent.

ALFRED: I don't know—I think I've seen enough of the blood of the recent violent trend in films.

WAKELIN: I'm not sure. I mean, I always have been an extreme pacifist, but recently I've begun to see the validity of violence. It's like my writing. I got so pissed off the other day when I tried writing and I sat there staring at a piece of paper and couldn't write because I felt "content." I mean, all the time when my life had been emotionally turbulent and turmoil-riden all I wanted was to be rid of the pain. But it made me write well.

ALFRED: I don't think an artist needs to suffer to create—I think that's a misconception.

WAKELIN: Granted. There are some fine writers and painters and others who can create of beauty and felicity. I just think, for myself, I've had a lot more pain than euphoria, and I really need pain to write well. I mean, I stared at the paper, at what I'd written before, and couldn't go on because I felt too good. Or not good, content. When I feel really good I can write too—but it's rarer than the pain. It's this nothingness—this god-awful contentedness that bothers the shit out of me. I need intense emotions to write. I want to survive fantastic highs and fantastic lows. And each time I survive an extreme and process it through writing—then I'm much more prepared to sink even lower or rise even higher. Do you know what I mean?

ALFRED: Yes, but I don't think it's fair to assume that all art must come out of intensity.

WAKELIN: For me it's necessary. I'm nothing when I'm content. A benign vegetable. And the art I admire comes out of extreme pain.

ALFRED: But don't you think art has a responsibility to provide answers for the pain, not just show it.

WAKELIN: What, by moralizing the artist's private answers? I hate this moralizing shit in literature.

ALFRED: No. I mean offering solutions for each small-scale Armageddon. A way out. One way out. It doesn't have to be the only way.

WAKELIN: Maybe. I prefer just the description of pain—its manifestations and ilk. Seeing this kind of intensity written by someone else causes an empathy between author and reader, providing both have a like outlook. If not, the reader won't find any value anyway. This empathy would cause me as a reader to understand the pain better, perhaps alleviating it through the understanding of its cause. Or if not, the literature is a fine solace. I think this is very important. The greatest purpose of any art form is making a person who is in pain see that pain is valuable. To learn through it. I think I've had more than my share of pain, but I wouldn't have it any other way. It made me intensely aware of myself.

ALFRED: Isn't that a high price to pay though, for self-knowledge?

WAKELIN: Well, if it's possible any other way, great. But I haven't seen that. There's so much pain—for everyone. It can be dismissed, it can be turned outwards, or it can be turned inwards. Turning it inwards is the hardest but I think, ultimately, the most valuable towards a person's uniqueness. Dismiss it, and we'd all run around similarly content. Turn it outwards, and we'd all be killers without conscience. Turn it inwards, and we'd each see who we really are. It makes thinking people instead of blissful ignorants.

chapter sixteen

QUESTION: WHAT IS ALL YOU SEED?

WAKELIN: DISCONTENT WITH MINIMAL EXISTENCE.

QUESTION: HOW?

WAKELIN: BY FINDING VALUE IN INTENSITY.

QUESTION: EVEN PAIN?

WAKELIN: YES.

QUESTION: AND LOVE?

WAKELIN : YES.

QUESTION: AND SANITY? OR INSANITY?

WAKELIN: YES, BOTH. IN EVERYTHING.

QUESTION: YET YOU LACK LOVE AND SANITY, OR PROPER INTENSITY THEREOF?

WAKELIN: PROPER INTENSITY THEREOF?

☢

The innocent is working at his high school radio station. He is now a sophomore in high school. His name is Jim.

He would go on to work for his college radio station until his license expired. He would be too lazy to ever renew it and would not work in radio again.

Jim has heard a rumor—one that had been obscurely newsworthy. He is compelled to share it over the air.

Wakelin, four years after his disappearance, has been seen in New Orleans. Reportedly, the drummer in Wakelin's Hinge has been down to New Orleans and has substantiated the rumor. A new album will be released soon.

This is all Jim has heard.

☢

The innocent returns from Los Angeles. No one greets him at the airport. He drives home alone, wanting to see his apartment again. His maroon touch-tone telephone greets him as he enters.

A conversation. Brief.

"Did you meet Wakelin?" The question is sarcastic.

"No, but I think I heard his voice. It may just have been my imagination."

Jim looks around his apartment. He has hung two large flags upon its walls—those of Albania and Haiti.

He remembers having heard that Haiti was the world's poorest nation. For this he sought to champion its cause. Likewise Albania—for he saw it as the only nation to defend the purity of Marxism-Leninism. He admires Enver Hoxha.

The innocent has had much to drink on the return flight. He sits down on his bed, closes his eyes, and his thoughts conquer him.

He thinks that Wakelin will someday find him and call him to follow. He imagines that he and eleven others are called to follow

Wakelin as he "retraces his lonesome steps."

What would he do for Wakelin? If Wakelin wanted, anything. Jim decides he would give himself to Wakelin in any requested manner.

Jim opens his eyes, finds his book on Shamanism, and reads a little.

He realizes that he hopes the experience he is to face in following Wakelin is intense. He desires to see Dante's *Inferno* and utopia, and he knows Wakelin will lead him there.

Jim finds dusk-colored boots, shirt, and pants. He dons them and feels he wants to go out drinking and evangelizing quietly to himself and the curious in some far-away corner.

He knows that Wakelin is alive.

chapter seventeen

QUESTION: WHAT I S ALL YOUR DEED?
WAKELIN: LIFE.
QUESTION: WHAT WAS ITS VALUE?
WAKELIN: I LEARNED, BUT NOT ENOUGH.
QUESTION: DID YOU FIND PROPER INTENSITY IN LIFE?
WAKELIN: I FOUND PROXIMITY TO DEATH.

Wakelin sits at a desk in his hotel room. His notebook is open before him. A pen lies atop it. His black handwriting fills the page with a geometric organization: diagonal margins perpendicular to triple-looped series of letters; comb-like lines occasionally ending as the paper does—sometimes finding their ways beyond the immediate plane onto the askew sheets of paper beneath. It matters little. Wakelin is merely emptying himself, not attempting coherency or extant infinity. Armageddon approaches, and his words here born are stillborn.

Wakelin shovels the bodies of the slain into endless trenches—graves of the abandoned.

Wakelin lights a cigarette, sits back, and reads what he has written. It all seems viable. He reads the blueprints for his own death.

His leaving the Hinge had been the precursor. What had been a theatre-piece has now been actualized. He had been oblique in describing his necessary departure, but it had been described. Few knew. Even fewer would find him again. So many blindmen running into walls.

Wakelin would die for all but the few. These would see that he would return from exile, an exile seemingly death. Wakelin does not smile. He does not show emotion. He is sullen and averted.

His steed takes him from the place where he has been Wakelin. Wakelin is dead—he has seen to it. He rides the whitewater; he rides his stallion away from this place. He rides.

They will say he is dead. The insipid saline coroners will achieve the voyeur's gratification in necrophilic thoughts. But the corpse they find will not be Wakelin's. Wakelin knows he lives still.

chapter Eighteen

QUESTION: YOU DESIRE THE INTENSITY OF DEATH?
WAKELIN: YES.
QUESTION: PROCEED THEN, deaddeaddeaddead.

☢

Beware the centipede that comes to crawl over your flesh.

Beware the death.

The pain of childbirth manifests itself once more in death—fetus opening itself in the fire. The stench of burning flesh. Smoke blinds the eyes of those who might have seen.

Viper-like, the child awakens, rearing up and staring at carnivores. Unafraid, for it has known non-birth, it walks away and renounces itself.

It enters a room and sets it ablaze, for all the child has seen of life is flame. It is consumed.

This was the savior they had all awaited.

Beware the centipede that comes to crawl over your flesh.

Beware the death.

☢

Centipede springs up from out of the unlit hallway. It is night and the mind is ripe.

Its emaciated face grins, bulging eyes aglow. Behind it stand its kin, in ranks nine wide and endlessly deep. All appear as the first—void of any dissimilar face—their silken robes colorless.

Wakelin regards the creatures as he retains his ground before them.

He begins to hear music. Its volume increases until he recognizes it. It is the score to his musical theatre-piece, "The Million-Year Centipede." Centipede and its kin begin a wild dance, gyrating in perfect time to the odd tempo and time signature changes of the piece. They begin to dance in formation toward Wakelin.

Wakelin tries to back away from the maniacal army he sees but is immobile.

Centipede reaches him first and, with a slight touch, knocks him over. Wakelin cannot cry out nor stand up. Centipede walks by, and its kin encircle Wakelin, row after row, kicking and trampling him in their dance. Row upon row repeat this ritual. Wakelin feels the pain at first, but grows accustomed to it. The music plays over and over for Centipede's infinite kin. Wakelin begins to think this so natural that he wonders if perhaps he has known no other existence than this. He soon forgets this thought, convinced of it. His vague recollections he dismisses as dreams.

He wonders if he can find pleasure in this experience. He realizes he can.

Simultaneously, music and dancers disappear.

☙

Centipede assumes human form. Languid but female, Centipede sits across the room on the bed. Wakelin puts a record on his turntable. He sits down on a chair facing the bed.

His apathy equals hers. The only difference—he enjoys the music he hears.

"Isn't this great music?"

☢

"It's okay."

He makes no mention of the fact that it is his own music—the last song of his last album.

She doesn't know Wakelin for who he is, or doesn't care. The music ends. Wakelin picks up his classical guitar and drunkenly plays a song only he's ever heard.

He finishes the song and leaves the room.

☢

Wakelin feels angry and depressed (WHICH? THEY ARE SYN-ONYMOUS). He swallows a bottle's worth of aspirin and finishes his beer.

Nine or ten months have passed since he was in the hospital due to an overdose of sleeping pills.

He wishes he had some now. But he is young and has much to accomplish.

He opens another beer.

He is now dead and cries out—

"Centipede! Must I suffer for my art? Must I die for it?"

YOU HAVE.

"When? I don't remember..."

Wakelin sees a telephone and stumbles toward it. He picks up the receiver, but it disintegrates in his hand.

He rushes out of his door and stands atop the stairs. He pauses. The pines and firs below reach up to embrace him. He sees their love and dives off to prove his own love.

Centipede tells him all this will be his.

⁕

Centipede?

    Will I find the intensity of love?

Cursed

      dying.

        I prostrate

my soul   soulless

  dead. Pain in falling—

                into

love. Falling falling

    failing to sustain

             love

             is

             pain.

Voyage the voyeur

             unknown to the

             unknown to the

             unknown.

To the unknown.

        Failsafe failing lifeless life.

               Sustenance

The Million-Year Centipede

is

Where is?

492832631223285279

late night loners

a shield protecting warrior emotions

runs amuck astride steeds

of: whitepure desires

in bloodblack minds:

Claws eaten by suicides

cannibals

come to crawl

HEREHEREHEREHERE

unsee passed

never reaching love.

NEVER

REACHING. reaching

after no

thing   person

thingthingthing

DESTROY

COMMAND: DESTROY BE DESTROYED DESTROY

BE DESTROYED COMMAND :

COMMAND.

Apathy should intense

A pathetic shoulder

for the dancer of the stallion

the dancer who   murdersdies

parescumparibus

facillime?congregantur

where?

Be afraid to lose and win

Be afraid to love and hate

SolidifySolace

Afraid.

of   of

of

where?HERE

self

murdersdiesmurders

DIES.DIES

COMMAND: DIE.

inflagrate conflagrate

in   KILL

I was set on fire

my hair burns

stench of burning flesh

quelch it with blood

COMMAND: BE CAREFUL NOT TO DROWN

quelch it with blood

quelch it with blood

and feel it.

you should have known what

I meant

ought to have known.

and feel it:

I am dying

for you all.

The dancers return. They carry buckets of blood and fire. Centipede strips Wakelin of his garments and gives him a silken robe, color-less as the rest.

Wakelin puts it aside as he sees the dancers emptying their buckets into a large basin. Centipede washes Wakelin in it. He then hands the robe to Wakelin. Wakelin puts it on the floor, steps into it, and lifts it up around himself so that it may hang from his shoulders.

"Centipede! Where am I?"

YOU ARE ALONE.

Wakelin sees a telephone and stumbles toward it. He picks up the receiver. He recognizes it as his own phone. He puts it to his ear, but the phone does not seem to be working.

He looks up and realizes he is in his apartment.

He is naked. He finds his clothes on the floor and puts them on. He sees his wallet and shoves it into his back pocket. He decides he needs a drink and leaves the apartment, hoping to find a bar nearby.

chapter Nineteen

WAKELIN STARES AT THE bloody mary that rests in front of the girl who sits next to him at the bar. His own drink has remained untouched.

He sees small arms reaching up out of the glass with hands trying to clutch at something unnameable. One of the hands reaches the edge of the glass and holds on to it. It rests awhile, then another hand, its twin, works its way next to it. The two pull together, attempting to free an unknown body from its liquid bondage. The glass is set unbalanced and rocks a little. The hands lose their grip and fall back into the glass.

"No!" cries Wakelin. He grabs the glass and empties its contents onto the bar, wanting to free its captives.

"What the fuck did you do that for?"

Wakelin is startled. He hasn't noticed anyone else. He looks at the girl next to him.

"Nothing. I hate bloody marys, that's all."

"Buy me another." The girl has shoulder-length dark wavy hair, a small mouth that seems incapable of demand, and large eyes that apparently contain the rings of Saturn.

"Leave me alone."

"Come on, clod. I want another."

"Here—have mine."

"What's in it?"

"I don't know. It's uninhabited."

She takes it and drinks a little.

"What's in it?" she repeats.

"Truth and beauty. Leave me alone."

"I want to know what the fuck's in this drink ... bartender!"

"Yeah, bartender, get me another."

"Another what?"

"Who gives a shit. Anything."

"Sure thing."

Wakelin turns to the girl.

"Hey, what day is it?"

"Thursday."

"Thursday what?"

"The fifth of November."

"Thanks."

Neither says anything for a while. The bartender brings Wakelin a screwdriver.

"So that's what this is."

"Maybe."

"Oh, fuck you."

Wakelin smiles briefly.

"What's that? A smile? I don't believe it. What are you smiling at?"

"Nothing." Wakelin thinks a little. "What you said."

"What? 'Fuck you'?"

"Huh?"

"I mean it, you know."

"What?"

"Let's go."

"Let me finish my drink."

"Well, do it fast."

Wakelin finishes his drink.

They leave and walk to his apartment.

chapter twenty

HOVERING ITS DEATH-BREATH above the soul of Wakelin, his soulless mind convinces him to deny what he desires.

Assume the worst.

Though it could be, there is no love here. Nor can there be.

The color of his room dissipates, its forms melting together to form a small liquid nothingness perfect in its structure.

This nothingness becomes substance and grows torrentially.

It leaves the room, always to return, to claim the death of a torment.

Wakelin commands it.

Sending it off, he realizes only that he is ridding himself of it, ignorant of the consequences, fearful of its return.

It is this small liquid nothingness that hunts torment as a sacrifice to the Centipede for Wakelin that is itself Wakelin's greatest torment.

chapter twenty-one

THE SPACESHIP HAS BEEN made very comfortable for Wakelin's sake. The plastic furniture that dominates the living-quarters, though not plush, is well-contoured to accommodate the human body.

It travels through consciousness at .2 of c destined only for travel. On the oblong plastic table rest three place settings and a half-dozen flasks of Zinfandel. Arrayed around the floral center-piece are various festal meats. Wakelin awaits his guests.

Wakelin sits down at the well-laden table and closes his eyes. He realizes he is trembling slightly. He opens his eyes again in order to find his cigarettes. He pulls an already lit one from the pack.

The lights turn out. The faint red glow from the burning ciga-rette consumes Wakelin's sight.

The lights remain out. As Wakelin stares at the fogged crimson, the smoke it emits begins to fill the room. It is a phosphorescent smoke subliminally emerald in its origins. Overwhelmingly, though, it echoes the hue of the screams of the ember cigarette.

Behind the other two place-settings sit the awaited visitors. Wakelin sees them. A canine-appearing Standenin Thuhrayn. A pale, sickly Gilbert Fishrising's replacement. Wakelin is neither surprised nor curious. They are here, as they are supposed to be.

Wakelin offers a salutatory toast to their freedom from the twenty-three types of boredom.

All boredom stems from the future.

The eight intellectual boredoms produced by knowledge of what will happen: repetition, premonition, commonplace, consistency, emptiness, retribution, samsara, erudition.

The eight bodily boredoms produced by reaction to what will happen: procrastination, anticipation, reconstruction, ennui, accumulation, exile, exhumation, extirpation.

The seven emotional boredoms produced by internalization of what will happen: indifference, loneliness, disappointment, rejection, acidity, alienation, deracination.

Gilbert Fishrising's replacement looks up into Wakelin's dark eyes, which are heavily browed as if shrouded in the mystique of prophecy.

"Disintegration," Gilbert Fishrising's replacement proffers. "Disintegration is boredom."

"What is its relationship to the future?" Wakelin asks, as he pours another glassful for his guests and himself.

"The future disintegrates, and is now disintegrating, as is everything else."

"Yes." Wakelin agrees, with a large swallow of wine in concordance. "Meanwhile eat and drink." Wakelin decides to begin his feasting with rabbit.

Gilbert Fishrising's replacement complies, attempting an entire leg of lamb. "Disintegration," he continues "is basic to everything. Even your boredoms disintegrate, yet, through such, it would seem that disintegration is itself an even greater boredom—provided one has knowledge, reaction, or internalization of it."

"Shiva," mutters Standenin Thuhrayn, vaguely projecting a nuzzled smile.

"Yeah, kind of." Gilbert Fishrising's replacement thinks that they'll never really understand. He wonders if perhaps these two strangers are robots or fish. Perhaps they are welders. He shudders in disgust. His revulsion is overcome momentarily in a glass of red wine, violently drunk. What occurs to him is to question why he is here, but the thought is quickly dismissed.

chapter twenty-two

THE INNOCENT AWAITS HIS guests.

The room is somewhat stuffy, but the innocent decides not to open the window to the -17° wind-chill factor outside.

A large silkscreen poster of Wakelin is hung from the top of some bookshelves in the center of the studio apartment.
The new album spins around, silent and waiting for a larger audience, on the turntable.

December in Wilmette is shit, the innocent decides. He'd never asked to live in Illinois. It just happened.

He reflects that it is more than slightly odd that a supposed collection of "previously unreleased older material" has been released as an album a little less than three years shy of a decade after Wakelin's exile. Released just in time for Wakelin's 35th birthday.

Tonight is the night of destruction. The innocent must again get sick. It is for Wakelin.

Lust flows torrentially.

Disruption for Wakelin.

A grinning silkscreen poster regards the decadence approvingly.

The innocent drinks and dances alone around the populated apartment.

A joint is passed. He dances as he accepts it. The combination tends to make him ill, but shit—it's Wakelin's birthday.

He plays the new Hinge album again.

The centipede calls farewell, forbidding thought as war.
   Knee-deep. Knee-deep.
   Beware the centipede that comes to crawl over your flesh.
   Beware the death.

chapter twenty-three

R. SIDENT COMES HOME after a day of working at the bookstore. He takes off his coat and rewinds the answering machine. As it rewinds, he finds an old envelope and a pencil. He turns the envelope over, face-down, and listens to the messages, prepared to write any of them down.

A few calls from friends. A message from his editor at *The Chicago Salmagundi* who publishes R.'s fiction and poetry. He wants R. to find someone at Lake Forest College, which R. attended until he took his leave of absence, to do a monthly review of the arts scene at LFC for the magazine.

R. ignores the phone calls when he hears the strange ones.

Sexy: "Hi there. I'll call you later if that's okay with you. Bye."

Desperate, perhaps overdosed on drugs: "Dingdoctai. Where are you? (background laughter by another person) What's wrong? Why won't you call me? This is Janis. My number is 555-2700. Please call. Thank you."

Bemusedly perturbed: "Howdy fucker."

All three are the same female voice. The middle message confuses R. and he plays it again.

Dingdoctai? What does that mean. Maybe it's "things are tied." Or "think too tired." He can't clearly decipher it, though, no matter how often he hears it.

Two females are involved in this, he decides, hearing the background laughter.

Janis? I never knew a Janis.

He begins to consider who could have made these calls. The girl at the bar—she doesn't know my last name.

555-2700. 555 numbers are bogus. Watching television for a half an hour would tell you that.

Erin? It could have been her laughter in the background. Oh well, R. dismisses, I've been getting weird phone calls since I first got to LFC. Why should I figure it out now if I never could before?

He pours himself a glass of port and sits down at his desk to read a little.

Blood is truth. The truth of the centipede.

A prophet calls out in the darkness: Hear me, fear the centipede. He brings his blood on you. Hear me, fear the prophecy.

Blood is fate. The fate of the mindless deaf.

You must follow as I retrace my lonesome steps or perish in blood. I have come to warn you of the truth and of the fate.

Beware the centpede that comes to crawl over your flesh.

Beware the death.

❖

Someone had given R. a book of poems written by a man named Wakelin. R. reads the first, and the longest, "The Million-Year Centipede."

R. wonders what Wakelin meant. Blood, death, fire, exile. Vipers, centipedes, saviors, prophets.

Sounds like God gone subterranean. Or like something that crawls out from under a large stone, nocturnal and poisonous.

R. shudders a little. It's all horseshit. What I need are a few drinks. He leaves, hoping to run into someone he knows at the bar.

❖

As R. Sident drinks his first Campari and soda, a great sense of relief engulfs him. He drinks quickly and orders up another. Realizing he hasn't eaten all day, R. knows exactly how drunk he soon will be.

❖

The bitter taste of Campari leaves the bar with him. R. has decided to go home again, albeit filled with a sense of shudder from Wakelin.

Horseshit. I'm too drunk. It's the bitterness that makes one shudder. All those Campari and sodas. All that Campari.

He begins to feel slightly ill and stumbles up the steps to his apartment, his pace ever-quickening as he realizes his one true desire in life—finding his washroom.

He slams the door behind him and wobbles a run to the toilet. Horseshit. I'm going to be sick.

He shudders as the Campari starts to come up, tasting like soap.

Vaguely, R. remembers how, at LFC, he had been drunk and had been eating crackers which, in spite of his care, splintered onto the carpeting in his dorm room. He had dutifully picked them up and sucked them into his mouth. It had been a private game of sorts to suck them into his mouth. Until he had mistaken a small chunk of soap for a cracker remnant.

R. feels more Campari wanting to come up.

Soap.

He opens his eyes and looks down into the toilet bowl. How red the Campari is. Much redder than in the bar.

Briefly a thought crosses his mind that makes him afraid. Has the Campari torn open my stomach? Perhaps I am throwing up my blood.

He opens his eyes again. The toilet bowl is full. And overflowing.

R. flushes and the toilet responds angrily, doubling and redoubling the amount of overflow.

Too much soap.

R. pictures red suds beginning to form.

His stomach is not yet empty. He feels his hands and legs getting wet.

The tops of his hands. His wrists.

He brings one hand to his face. He brings the smell of blood. He wants to move, to leave the bathroom and its invisible carnage behind. Yet he cannot, he has not yet finished why he came here and, until he does, he dare not move.

The soap is gone—all is now blood. He is to stay here, he will stay till he drowns in blood—the blood he vomits like the truth spewed forth by prophets.

R. recalls "The Million-Year Centipede." He knows.

The cold ache that pulses through one's body, that courses its way through one's head, the cold ache that follows retching was welcomed.

It was a dry ache, yet a glorious one.

R. opens his eyes again. There is no blood, no Campari, no overflow. The water in the toilet is still. R. opens his eyes and knows.

He is to live.

He will stay till Wakelin comes.

chapter Twenty-Four

WAKELIN CLOSES HIS EYES and listens to Standenin Thuhrayn speak of his pain in human society.

Wakelin is thrust back into so much he'd prefer not being thrust back into. He isn't drunk, but he feels he should be. There are twenty-three types of boredom. He listens until Standenin Thuhrayn is finished to explain them to him and to Gilbert Fishrising's replacement, who Wakelin knows still questions disintegration in regards to the boredom axioms.

☙

Run.   On the run.

away... away

The steed, the

white steed.

Merge.

The steed of death.

chapter twenty-five

REPETITION.

Seething repetitions.

They made Wakelin see a psychiatrist after his misdemeanor: attempted suicide.

Repetition compulsion. Destined unchange resulting from destined need to repeat.

Psychiatrist repeating: yours is a repetition compulsion, yours is a repetition compulsion.

Wakelin: I woke up—I changed. Painful awareness.

Premonition.

Dream:

Entering the doorway of the previous year's Janet's dorm room, Wakelin met a man he didn't recognize. Wakelin asked him who he was. The reply: Janet's boyfriend from summer. Wakelin was irritated yet vented no frustration. Janet entered the room. She asked Wakelin if he was angry. He replied: of course not. Wakelin left it at that and left. The room was located across the hall from the room she had actually lived in the year before.

Wakelin then planned the murder of Janet. An underworld expert was hired to provide him with an automobile with which he could either lure or force Janet's car into a tree at high speed. Wakelin's car was capable of extreme speed as well as amazing maneuverability. Were he luring or forcing Janet's car into the tree, Wakelin could easily swerve away in time.

This whole while Wakelin's body had not been Wakelin's. Wakelin was in the body of a man named Jay, who had shared a geology class with Janet and Wakelin in the previous spring and with whom, on field expedition, Wakelin had gotten drunk (peppermint schnapps and beer), as well as stoned, to Janet's displeasure.

Final preparations were made on the car. Wakelin inspected it and noticed his tobacco pipe connected to the frame or underhood innards of the vehicle. An additional weapon, perhaps related to a catapult of sorts, the pipe either served as the catapult or as a trigger mechanism therefor. Wakelin and vehicle in a state of preparation, Wakelin was ready to leave on his mission of murder.

Alarm: 6:30 A.M. Wakelin was frightened and shaken at the implications of the dream. His roommate told him he'd been speaking German in his sleep: maggots and mud.

Wakelin phoned Janet and woke her, wondering if something had happened to her. She was perturbed by the disturbance.

⁂

Commonplace.

Yes? You're much too common for me…

Wakelin, half drunk or more so, swayed as he attempted to yank up the lid to the toilet. It came up with a crash and bounced back down again. Wakelin, not easily discouraged, attempted it again and succeeded. He opened his fly and simultaneously looked into the toilet.

Someone had forgotten to flush down his shit.

Wakelin looked at his feet while he pissed and saw another pile of shit on the floor only inches from his feet. He might, hadn't some form of luck been in his favor, have stepped in it.

Consistency.

Appendages in concordance.

A cost, and herded file had effroyable advancement contracts, realized nigh, and picnics.

It was for this.

"Let. Let me out. Find locks."

"We had assurance, road darkness. This and I had stories for them."

Late night rain carried Wakelin home.

"Sleep naked and let me out."

They've never understood the stories.

Emptiness.

Void.

Wakelin's mind wandered with one primary thought as its focus: away. Away from here.

Ponder: where is here. Ponder: where is not here.

104

Elsewhere. Elsewhereness. Wakelin desired this above all.

He saw it. An outer space deep within himself that contained nothing and was contained by nothing.

Wakelin struggled and found himself concentrating more on struggling than on the outerspace deep within himself.

Wrong, he thought, No concentration. Wander.

He wandered farther and saw a spaceship but ignored it.

No spaceships, he thought. Wander Away.

When he lost here, Wakelin found he was nowhere and knew he had passed by what he had been looking for.

It, the spaceship he realized had been important, had been the outer space deep within himself. It had been a flickering image which would have carried him away from even that important region.

Wakelin had been caught in a space.

Retracing, he sought the spaceship again, but it was no longer there, had it ever been.

All that was there was now here, and that was the outer space deep within himself which was no longer an outer region or an inner one. It was space, and he had been trapped in it.

☢

Retribution.

The elegiac distich makes apparent the erotic ecstacy of the funeral song.

Times occur within a life when lovers love the dead without asking why. Ten days live that time forgot when communion was served among the dying and her (She was one) whom Wakelin came to love.

Wakelin came, but then, too, he left, for lack of timelessness. Death grinned and tried to ignore him, but he, he knew the truth. Love cannot live among the nondecomposed dead.

⁂

Samsara.

Cycle of existence.

Wakelin was Skom, a man unable to die, a man who had wanted to die for pain but had not been permitted death.

There was something in wandering alone through a city.

There was something in death, but it never came.

There was something in everything.

⁂

Erudition.

Wakelin sat in the back of the classroom. Occasionally he'd look up and try to discover what was being discussed. Cetology in Melville. Ambergris.

Wakelin focused back on his thoughts. He gazed at the sheet of paper which held the potential for an unwritten poem entitled *House on Fire*. He and two proselytes often took to cowriting poetry by alternating lines.

1st Proselyte: When is life sad?

2nd Proselyte: Mounting depression,

Wakelin: Enveloping a human regression

1st Proselyte: Involving the extreme contradictions of hatred,

2nd Proselyte: Lacking all reason,

Wakelin: And destroying the fundament of human sanity,

1st Proselyte: Existing only in the realm of space,

2nd Proselyte: Existing without meaning,

Wakelin: For earth is space and doesn't matter,

1st Proselyte: Existence is empty and doesn't matter,

2nd Proselyte: As we intone space and uphold an

Wakelin: Aphonic bond.

1st Proselyte: We all could rejoice

2nd Proselyte: And project ourselves on the firmament

Wakelin: As we experience the silent cessation.

chapter twenty-six

WAKELIN PAUSES, HE GLANCES at Standenin Thuhrayn and at Gilbert Fishrising's replacement. Their images fade.

Wakelin is no longer aboard the spacecraft. He is kneeling in front of Centipede. Centipede is alone, sitting on a marble throne.

Wakelin, not wanting to see, looks at the floor.

"Centipede?"

"Why have you paused?"

"Am I right? Is what I say true?"

Centipede laughs. The laughter makes Wakelin shudder.

Wakelin is a voyeur, seeing his dreams and drawing life from them.

He sees the kin of Centipede, the dancers, making love to a hundred lovers he had had. He sees the mournful, tear-streaked faces scourged of all traces of self-piety. Wakelin smiles. He knew all would come to this.

Wakelin sees the convergence of fire and blood.

Wakelin hears the hissing deaths of blindmen.

⁂

The innocent, the man named Jim, cries out for Wakelin. He calls for truth and the vision.

"Bring him to me," Wakelin tells Centipede. "Let me speak with him."

"His time has been predetermined. You must continue. The pause has been harmful."

"Should he not hear this also?"

"He knows most of what you've never said. Let him be until his time has come."

chapter Twenty-seven

PROCRASTINATION.

Deference.

Wakelin had had a cigarette and his hands were shaking. He looked around the dormitory's study room. Standing up, he glanced at the books arranged and neatly rearranged on the table in front of him. The blank notebook paper admonished him.

A comparison of the concept of suicide as expressed in the writings of David Hume and Plato. He knew the paper had to be written within a few hours. He knew he had to support Hume. Plato's condemnation stared at Wakelin shallowly while he contemplated his own words.

Wakelin frowned. He left the study and went downstairs into his own room. He got a bottle of wine out of his refrigerator, opened it, and poured himself a glass. He sat down on his bed. Wakelin stood up again and walked over to his closet.

Seven years before, a student who had lived in the dormitory had corresponded with his girlfriend in Colorado. Her letters spoke of her concern over a sexual experience they had shared.

For whatever reason, the letters had been discarded in the basement. Wakelin had found them.

"My mother and I had quite a long discussion last night. She had found my 'pills' so I had to just tell her the truth about everything—even Chicago. Well god, your parents know about it, so why should I continue to keep it from my mother? She has an amazing ability to find things out anyway—I'm glad I told her."

Wakelin decided this was more important that Hume. He read more.

☢

Anticipation.

Five o'clock a.m. Wakelin rolled over. He was temporarily freed from his pregustant nightmare: he travels along a road, walking toward an important destination; he stops, having forgotten why he was going there.

Alcohol has left Wakelin dry, dusty. His thirst woke him up.

He sat up in his bed, regaining focus while deciding if all he wanted was water—it was ten feet to the bathroom, fifty to the kitchen.

Then he remembered the bottle of Alsatian beer. He opted for the kitchen.

Returning with his beer, he turned on the television and sat in the chair opposite it. The volume was turned off—Wakelin left it off. He watched computerized farm reports—the screen filled with words and numbers.

He smelled the drying blood but ignored it.

Wakelin had seen the dark pulsation of the Sea of Death and he knew today he would enter it.

He turned off the television and found a copy of a book entitled *A Season in Hell*. He opened it but decided he didn't feel like reading. He dropped the book to the floor, knowing he'd pick it up and read it later.

Wakelin went back to bed, but he couldn't sleep. He lay awake and remembered, as a small child, he'd often cried at not having been able to sleep, and his tears had opened the doors of panic. It was as if sleep were a measureable achievement.

Reconstruction.

Rising airplane way / place.

Rule blood.

      Storm. Smile receiver-like

into the past.

Standing out bottle:

To drink; drunk—telephone beckoning voices.

      Storm. Smile receiver-like

into Janet.

"Hello, is Janet there?"

"No, she's gone for the whole semester."

Wakelin hadn't seen her in well over a year and a half (excluding crashing a party at her sorority, drunk and unaccountable).

"Oh. I'll call her later, I guess."

"Yeah, like next year."

⚛

Ennui.

Arthur Rimbaud (*A Season in Hell*): "Et je redoute l'hiver parce que c'est la saison du confort!"

There is nothing in life but drinking and weeping.

⚛

Accumulation.

There were a lot of drugs inside Wakelin, working against each other to destroy him. White cross against valium; alcohol against dope. Alcohol to calm himself, dope to get himself high, valium to come down, white cross to stay awake.

Wakelin looked at the line of coke and paused. He took his straw out of an empty drink, shook it dry, and snorted the coke. The Hinge was waiting for him on a darkened stage. He stumbled to meet them and started to shiver. Shakily, he strapped on his guitar.

The lights went on—Wakelin stared at the screaming audience. He screamed back.

"Listen. Hey listen. Listen, man. We're going to do you all some good this evening. Listen: I'm going to tell you a story."

The band began to play, Wakelin not *noticing* his *own* guitar work.

The son of a pusher told me to go down to the bar, to buy myself some whiskey and a brand new car, to buy myself a woman, to buy myself a girl, to buy myself a coat-of-arms, to buy myself a world. I bought myself these and all the rest. I bought myself my death.

Beware the centipede that comes to crawl over your flesh. Beware the death.

❖

Exile.

Wakelin once had a girlfriend named Karen. She was quite a bit younger than he and less tolerant.

He had given her his poetry to read.

Wakelin had been active in a church during his high school years, but found himself forced out of the youth group he in part led due to embarrassments which arose. He had at times revealed too much of himself to female members of the group during emotional intimacy (false intimacy, as he discovered later). He was labeled depressive and was outcast.

Wakelin found a different church, a different youth, in which to involve himself. When he found most of the girls attracted to him, he chose for himself the most vociferous.

However, his decision was only made possible through many poems, in which he explored the possibilities of relationships with each of the more vociferous.

These poems were among the collected works he showed Karen. It was enough to frighten her away.

❖

Exhumation.

Wakelin's first lover had been named Lynn, a short dark-haired girl he had met in college.

They had been engaged, but Lynn, who had initially suggested the engagement, changed her mind. Instead, she stole some posters from Wakelin and continued to attempt to widen the Panama Canal.

She was the first to die, to drown.

Wakelin had found her body, maggot-infested and filled with the blood of purgatory truth.

⁘

Extirpation.

Wakelin: the captive rode in the back seat of his parents' Pontiac, traveling west through Iowa at ninety miles an hour along U.S. Highway 20.

He pushed his door open and closed it again.

"What are you doing?"

"It wasn't closed right."

"What are you, insane? Don't you know how dangerous that is? I never want you to open the door again when we're on the god-damn highway, you understand?"

Wakelin fell silent for a minute ("what are you, insane? what are you, insane? what are you, insane?").

"I'll show you fucking insane."

Wakelin pushed the door open again and dove out. He ignored the pain in his shoulder, got up, climbed over the barbed fence alongside the road, and ran across the field there with one primary thought: away.

chapter twenty-eight

WAKELIN PAUSES.

He closes his eyes.

A few minutes pass. He opens his eyes: another place-setting, another guest: R. Sident has joined them.

R. Sident: "I recall 'The Million-Year Centipede.' I know." Wakelin offers a toast. He looks at Gilbert Fishrising's replacement. "Freedom from disintegration."

Standenin Thuhrayn: "Freedom."

Gilbert Fishrising's replacement smiles at Wakelin: "The seven emotional boredoms."

chapter twenty-nine

INDIFFERENCE.

Evil in the skull.

Wakelin sat down in front of his closet door. The lights were off, save for those of his receiver. He was listening to the ugliest music he could find, savoring the dissonance of primal scream.

Wakelin took a gulp of his medicine-bottle concoction: brandy, sherry, scotch, rum, madeira. He had taken a little of each so that his parents wouldn't notice their diminished supply.

Sandlewood incense and scented candles decorated his room.

Wakelin's mind withdrew into dissonance.

Considerations: murder / suicide.

Wakelin held his eyelids open until his eyes watered. He concentrated on the sensation of tears responding to gravity. His eyes stung as he let down his lids. The side of the record had come to an end. The tone-arm did not reject, and Wakelin sat still, listening to the repeating anapest of the last groove.

He fell asleep.

✛

Loneliness.

Wakelin went down to the liquor store and bought a quart of beer. He walked the two miles to the beach.

He sat on a bench, occasionally sipped from his brown bag, and watched some kids play Frisbee golf.

He saw others in the park drinking or taking drugs, but they all had their cars and their friends.

Wakelin had his quart of beer and smiled at this friend, this vehicle that moved his life from the city called Today to the ghost town called Tomorrow.

✛

Disappointment.

Wakelin entered an octagonal room. In each corner sat a bearded man. Each man chanted to himself.

Wakelin walked up to each in turn and asked the meaning of truth.

The first spit in Wakelin's face.

The second pissed on Wakelin's feet.

The third slit his wrists and smeared the blood on Wakelin's chest.

The fourth opened an infection and sprayed pus in Wakelin's eyes.

The fifth wept.

The sixth masturbated into orgasm.

The seventh perspired heavily.

The eighth vomited, died, and decomposed.

Wakelin sat in the middle of the room and lit himself on fire.

❖

Rejection.

Scorn lit from the brazier of Centipede: no time, no time, the seasons have come to banal conclusions.

Wakelin awoke and walked downtown. He was looking for something in store-front windows, in moving cars, in the eyes of pedestrians.

Wakelin was looking for something he never found.

❖

Acidity.

An urgency pervaded Wakelin's philosophy.

Wakelin, Ray Douer, and the Hinge drummer were drunk in the lobby of a hotel. Wakelin attempted to explain to them the urgency he felt.

They laughed and mocked him. They told him nothing would matter soon enough: silence was espousement of truths.

Wakelin cussed and called them blind.

"While I live, I see. While I see, I profess."

❖

Alienation.

Wakelin entered the fraternity house and looked for Janet. The party obstructed him, but eventually he found her downstairs, dancing with someone.

He walked up to the pair and asked if she'd break away to talk to him.

"I can't—I've committed myself for a few more dances."

Wakelin went upstairs to the bar and got embarrassingly drunk. He'd put up with enough.

He went back downstairs to find her.

"I can't—I've committed myself for a few more dances. These are my friends."

Wakelin caught the implication.

"Well, listen. You told me to come. If you're going to fucking ignore me, I'm leaving. See you."

Wakelin left, walked around upstairs, and then went outside. "What the fuck's going on?" he said to no one in particular. Wakelin went back to the bar, had a few more drinks, and wandered back downstairs.

"Listen, Janet. I'm leaving unless you'll talk to me for a while."

Silence.

"Fuck you."" Wakelin left.

☙

Deracination.

Anracunathon plenduum oernimor devancinati ovenminet qencuthatha qeratue qeramadr aqerumdorn.

chapter thirty

The Million-year Centipede

GREET THE SUPRACONSCIOUS, SEEKER. Greet the bloodstained hand which bids welcome to levels beneath your own. Enter not in fear, but in terror, for herein lies the secret which calls insanity home. Enter cautiously. Enter consciously, and you will perish in self. Abandon that which you've known, and enter anew and cleansed. Be purged of your uncleanliness by that entity which dwells in the deepest depth of the infinite space. Enter, and be wary. Distortion lights the way.

Beware the centipede that comes to crawl over your flesh. Beware the death.

In my mind the centipede crawls and dwells alone, aloof, lashing vehemently with tongue and fang. He buries to withdraw from you the remnants of some long-forgotten tribe—he is unalive—

Beware the centipede that comes to crawl over your flesh. Beware the death.

The Million-Year Centipede

Between your legs, between your dreams, he comes to slither past unseen, to leave his imprint on your soul, and bludgeon-feast from parts a whole. A creature knows creation-self and death beneath him's unimport, just wary be of sanity for it is mere illusory and spews on winds as sand-cast fort.

Beware the centipede that comes to crawl over your flesh. Beware the death.

Have you ever seen a centipede flattened against the wall? If you ever see a centipede, you'll see no one at all: they crawl across your mind at night and take the parts that are sane. Have you ever seen a centipede flattened against your brain? Once I was a small believer telling everybody else's pain. Now I know I'm ill with fever; now I know I've gone insane. Won't it please destroy your fate; won't it please stand still? Have you ever seen a centipede flattened against your will?

Three years shy of a decade I was forced to be away—an exile from the land of strength and sagacity and justice. Now I have returned, my friends. Sleep now, for tomorrow you must follow as I retrace my lonesome steps. Prepare yourselves. Beware the centipede that comes to crawl over your flesh. Beware the death.

The pain of childbirth manifests itself once more in death—fetus opening itself in the fire. The stench of burning flesh. Smoke blinds the eyes of those who might have seen.

Viper-like, the child awakens, rearing up and staring at carnivores. Unafraid, for it has known non-birth, it walks away and renounces itself.

It enters a room and sets it ablaze, for all the child has seen of life is flame. It is consumed.

This was the savior they had all awaited.

Beware the centipede that comes to crawl over your flesh. Beware the death.

The centipede calls farewell, forbidding thought as war. Knee-deep. Knee-deep.

Beware the centipede that comes to crawl over your flesh. Beware the death.

Blood is truth. The truth of the centipede.

A prophet calls out in darkness: Hear me, fear the centipede. He brings his blood on you. Hear me, fear the prophecy.

Blood is fate. The fate of the mindless deaf.

You must follow as I retrace my lonesome steps or perish in blood. I have come to warn you of the truth and of the fate.

Beware the centipede that comes to crawl over your flesh. Beware the death.

The son of a pusher told me to go down to the bar, to buy myself some whiskey and a brand new car, to buy myself a woman, to buy myself a girl, to buy myself a coat-of-arms, to buy myself a world. I bought myself those and all the rest. I bought myself my death.

Beware the centipede that comes to crawl over your flesh. Beware the death.

chapter Thirty-one

THE SPACESHIP MOVES TOWARD a forbidden sea—the Sea of Liquid. Wakelin is engulfed by spit and piss.

He is engulfed by blood. Pus.

Tears. Come. Sweat.

Vomit.

A torrent of water.

Death and decomposition.

Ether.

Gilbert Fishrising's replacement and Wakelin stand atop a mountain cliff surrounded by an ocean of blood.

Janet drowns beneath them.

They see an army of welders. The army also drowns.

This land had been known as Indiana.

Jim, the innocent joins Wakelin on the mountain. Gilbert Fishrising's replacement has gone.

"There was a woman. I told her about you. I told her I'd have to leave to find you. You know, I thought you were in L. A. You weren't. But I knew you were alive.

"I told her—I said 'I have to leave to find Wakelin.' She couldn't handle the scene. She told me I was messing with the devil."

"Was she right?"

"No."

They stare together at the forest of firs and pines.

"I've been waiting for you, Jim. This shit is yours now."

Five sit around the spaceship's banquet.

Wakelin lights a joint and the other four leave—Gilbert Fishrising's Replacement, Standenin Thuhrayn, B. Sident, Jim the Innocent.

Wakelin inhales deeply. He realizes they have gone to meet Centipede. They will know what to do.

Wakelin loved.

He loved. He had loved so fervently, so believingly. His love manifested itself in death. Because he loved, death embraced his life, and the two became as one: a monism built in an effort to please liquid structures, built upon the shedding of blood.

about the author

ECKHARD GERDES GREW UP among philistines who belittle all attempts to enrich our lives with literature and art. His work had to be covert, for the dominant culture seeks to silence all whose voices do not chant the dominant culture's desires in unison. He was able to pick up an MFA in writing from the School of the Art Institute of Chicago along the way, but not before one teacher threatened to choke Eckhard to death for producing this kind of writing. Eckhard's true teachers have been the voices he heard through literature—Brautigan, Patchen, Joyce, Beckett, Federman, Barth, Jaffe, Burroughs, Acker, Moorcock, Calvino, Ionesco, and the amazing Arno Schmidt to name a few—and the voices he has heard through other art forms, such as Clyfford Still, Picasso, Pollack, Kraan, Captain Beefheart, Pere Ubu, Stockhausen, Webern, and, of course, The Doors. These are the voices of the idiosyncratic. They will be heard long after the weak voices have faded.

He lives near Chicago with two of his sons, Ludwig and Ulysses. His oldest son, Sterling, is away at college at Georgia Tech. Occasionally, Eckhard publishes *The Journal of Experimental Fiction*. At times, he writes about literature for *The Review of Contemporary Fiction*, *American Book Review*, and *Electronic Book Review*. His fiction appears in various journals every now and then. *The Million-Year Centipede* is his sixth published novel.

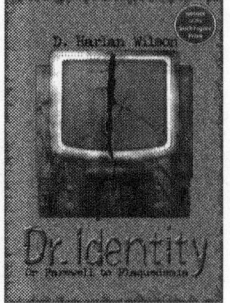